Arthur's Birthday Party

story and pictures by
Lillian Hoban

HarperCollins*Publishers*

HarperCollins®, 📖®, and I Can Read Book®
are trademarks of HarperCollins Publishers Inc.

Arthur's Birthday Party
Copyright © 1999 by Lillian Hoban
Printed in the U.S.A. All rights reserved.

Library of Congress Cataloging-in-Publication Data
Hoban, Lillian.
    Arthur's birthday party / story and pictures by Lillian Hoban.
        p.   cm. — (An I can read book)
    Summary: Arthur the chimpanzee is determined to be the best all-around
gymnast at his gymnastics birthday party.
        ISBN 0-06-027798-X. — ISBN 0-06-027799-8 (lib. bdg.)
    [1. Birthdays—Fiction.   2. Chimpanzees—Fiction.   3. Gymnastics—
Fiction.   4. Parties—Fiction.]   I. Title.   II. Series.
PZ7.H635Ab   1999   97-42225
[E]—dc21   CIP
                                                                                          AC

3   4   5   6   7   8   9   10

Visit us on the World Wide Web!
http://www.harperchildrens.com

For Ben, Daniel, Kobi, Elias, Ilana
and Alisa—
the best grandchildren ever

It was Saturday morning.

Arthur was making invitations
for his birthday party.

Violet and Wilma were taking turns
pushing each other on the swing.

"My big sister had a beach party
for her birthday," said Wilma.

"Everyone wore a bathing suit,
and there was
a Miss Bathing Beauty contest."

"That does not sound

like fun to me,"

said Arthur.

"At my party

there will be lots of fun."

"We had lots of fun
at Michelle's party,"
said Violet.
"We went to Old MacDonald's Zoo
and rode on a little train
and had lollypops."

"Old MacDonald's Zoo

is for babies,"

said Arthur.

"My party will be

for big kids only,

with no babies allowed."

"Can I come?"

asked Violet.

"I am not a baby."

"Huh," said Arthur.

"Only babies need to be pushed

on the swing.

Big kids know

how to swing themselves.

Watch me."

Arthur got on the swing

and pushed off.

He stuck his legs

straight up in the air

and pulled them back hard.

"See," he said.

"This is called pumping.

It's what big kids do."

"Well, Mr. Smarty,"

said Wilma,

"little kids know

how to pump too.

We were just playing

mamas and babies,

weren't we, Violet?"

"Yes," said Violet.

"We can pump on the swing,

and we can climb ropes too!"

"Well," said Arthur,

"I bet you can't do this."

Arthur pumped the swing up high.

He jumped off

and caught onto the rope.

Just then Norman rode up

on his bike.

"Arthur," he called,

"did you decide

what kind of party

you're having?"

Arthur climbed up the rope

and balanced on top

of the playset.

"Yes," he said.

"I just got a great idea.

I will have a gymnastics party.

There will be rope climbing

and balancing and tumbling

and a prize for the best gymnast."

"Oh, wow!" said Norman.

"I love gymnastics!

Can I bring my trampoline?

I can jump higher than anyone."

"Sure," said Arthur,

"but I bet I'm the best gymnast,

so I'll get the prize!"

"That's not fair,"

said Wilma.

"There should be separate prizes.

One for balancing,

and one for rope climbing . . ."

"And one for tumbling,"

said Violet.

"I tumble better than anyone

in my tumbling class."

"Maybe it *would* be good

to have prizes for different things,"

said Arthur.

"The prizes could be medals

made out of gold paper.

I'll still win the prize

for best all-around gymnast!"

"We'll see about that,"

said Wilma.

"Come on, Violet.

Let's go practice on my playset."

"I think I will practice

jumping on my trampoline,"

said Norman.

"Do you want to come, Arthur?"

"No," said Arthur.

"I don't need to practice."

Norman rode off on his bike.

Arthur finished making

the party invitations.

They said:

COME TO ARTHUR'S
GYMNASTICS BIRTHDAY PARTY
TIME: SATURDAY AT 3 O'CLOCK
PLACE: ARTHUR'S PLAYSET

Arthur put the invitations

into envelopes.

Then he went down the road

to deliver them.

When he got to Norman's yard,

he saw Norman practicing

on the trampoline.

Norman jumped way up in the air

and spun all the way around.

Arthur watched Norman

until he went into the house.

"That looked easy,"

said Arthur.

He got on the trampoline

and jumped as high as he could.

28

He tried to spin around,

but he fell flat on his face.

"Phooey," said Arthur.

"Well, maybe Norman will be

best on the trampoline,

but I will still be

best all-around gymnast."

Arthur walked down the road

to Wilma's house.

He looked through the fence.

He could see Wilma and Violet

at Wilma's playset.

Violet was tumbling,

and Wilma was swinging.

"Violet," called Wilma,

"Arthur is spying on us!"

"Are you, Arthur?"

asked Violet.

"No, I'm not," said Arthur.

"Besides, there is nothing

you can do

that I can't do better!"

He put Wilma's invitation

into her mailbox.

"See?" he said.

"I'm a good big brother.

I'm inviting your friend Wilma

so you won't feel bad

about not winning a prize,

because Wilma won't win one either!"

"Don't be so sure about that,"

said Violet.

Arthur delivered invitations

to John and Billy and Jimmy.

All that week

Violet went to Wilma's playset

to practice.

"Why can't you practice at home?"

asked Arthur.

"What's so special

at Wilma's playset?"

"Wilma's playset isn't special,"

said Violet.

"What I'm practicing is special."

"It can't be so special,"

said Arthur.

"It's just baby stuff."

"No it's not," said Violet.

"You'll see.

It's special and it's a secret,

so I can't tell you."

"Phooey," said Arthur.

"Little sisters always have secrets.

They are no fun."

All that week,

whenever Arthur asked

Norman to play,

Norman said,

"I can't.

I have to practice

on my trampoline."

"Phooey," said Arthur.

"Friends who practice

all the time are no fun."

Finally, it was Saturday.

At three o'clock

everyone came

to Arthur's birthday party.

They all had presents for Arthur.

"No opening presents
until you blow out the candles
on your birthday cake,"
said Violet.

"When do we get to do gymnastics?"

asked John.

"I want to be first!"

yelled Billy.

Then Jimmy and Norman yelled,

"I want to be first!"

"I want to be first!"

Wilma said,

"We don't care if we go

first or last, do we, Violet?"

"That's right," said Violet.

"Well," said Arthur,

"it's my birthday,

so I get to go first."

Arthur somersaulted

onto the trampoline.

"Now you are going to see

some great all-around gymnastics,"

he said.

Arthur jumped as high as he could.

He caught onto the rope

and climbed to the top.

Then he balanced across

the top of the playset.

"Now watch this," he said.

He hung from his hands

and swung back and forth.

Then he flipped between his arms,

jumped onto the slide,

and slid to the ground.

Everyone clapped and cheered.

49

Jimmy went next.

He twirled the rope

until it was all twisted.

Then he climbed to the top.

The rope untwisted

and Jimmy spun round and round.

"Ya-hoo, ya-hoo!" he yelled.

Everyone clapped and cheered.

They all clapped and cheered

for Billy when he balanced

on top of the playset,

and for Norman

when he did

a double spin

on the trampoline,

and for John

when he tumbled

and did backward flips.

Then Wilma said,

"Violet and I are going

to do TEAM gymnastics."

Wilma did a cartwheel.

She bent backward

and made an arch.

Violet took a running jump

and somersaulted

right through Wilma's arch.

"Yippee! Yippee!"

everyone cheered.

Arthur didn't say anything.

Then Violet jumped onto

Wilma's shoulders,

grabbed the rope,

and climbed to the top.

Violet slowly turned upside down.

She reached down to Wilma.

Wilma bounced up,

caught Violet's hand,

and swung to the top

of the playset.

Then Violet swung

herself up.

Both girls hung from their hands.

They flipped between their arms,

jumped to the ground,

and bowed.

"Yow-ee! Yow-ee!"

everyone cheered.

"Phooey!" said Arthur.

"It's not fair.

There's two of you

and only one of me."

"I think it's very fair,"

said Wilma.

"That's right," said Violet.

"Now everyone gets to win.

Jimmy wins for rope climbing.

Billy wins for balancing.

Norman wins for trampoline.

John wins for tumbling.

Wilma and I win

for team gymnastics.

And Arthur wins for

BEST ALL-AROUND GYMNAST."

"Just like I said I would!"

yelled Arthur.

So everyone got a prize.

Then Arthur blew out the candles

on his birthday cake

and opened his presents.

They all had pizza and cake
and ice cream.

And everyone said it was the
best birthday party ever.